Monkey
Business

To Katie, my love, and to my little chums
Calla, Sadie, Matthew and Harriet.

Many thanks to Jane F., Mike F. and Jenny C.

First paperback edition 2008

Kids Can Press acknowledges the financial support of the Government of
Ontario, through the Ontario Media Development Corporation's Ontario Book Initiative;
the Ontario Arts Council; the Canada Council for the Arts; and the Government
of Canada, through the BPIDP, for our publishing activity.

Published in Canada by   Published in the U.S. by
Kids Can Press Ltd.   Kids Can Press Ltd.
29 Birch Avenue   2250 Military Road
Toronto, ON M4V 1E2   Tonawanda, NY 14150

www.kidscanpress.com

The artwork in this book was rendered in watercolor, colored pencil and gouache.
The text is set in CrudFont.

Edited by Tara Walker
Designed by Julia Naimska
Printed and bound in China

The hardcover edition of this book is smyth sewn casebound.
The paperback edition of this book is limp sewn with a drawn-on cover.

CM 04 0 9 8 7 6 5
CM PA 08 0 9 8 7 6 5 4 3 2 1

Library and Archives Canada Cataloguing in Publication

Edwards, Wallace

Monkey business / Wallace Edwards.

ISBN 978-1-55337-462-6 (bound)   ISBN 978-1-55453-228-5 (pbk.)

1. English language — Idioms — Juvenile literature.
I. Title.

PE1460.E48 2004   j428   C2004-900410-7

Kids Can Press is a LORUS™ Entertainment company

Monkey Business

Wallace Edwards

Kids Can Press

IDIOM: a group of words whose meaning cannot be understood from the meaning of the individual words; an expression, peculiar to a specific language, that cannot be translated literally

Even in a serious meeting, Professor Apeson sensed there might be monkey business going on.

When he was on the ball, there was no limit to what King Pigglebottom could do.

It was cold and wet outside, but Gavin felt as snug as a bug in a rug.

Although Mumford had promised not to gossip, he let the cat out of the bag.

"Not again," sighed Owen. "It isn't easy being a bull in a china shop."

Eloise had a craving for snails, but she accidentally opened a can of worms.

Phil had no formal musical training,
so he learned to play by ear.

Quentin could always be counted on to rise to the occasion.

Sometimes, thought Camellia, it's better to show your true colors.

Forbes had no intention of sharing his
cupcake — he had a real sweet tooth.

When it was time to deliver, Peg laid
it on the line.

"'Tis a dog-eat-dog world," mused Reginald,
reflecting on his life of hard-won luxury.

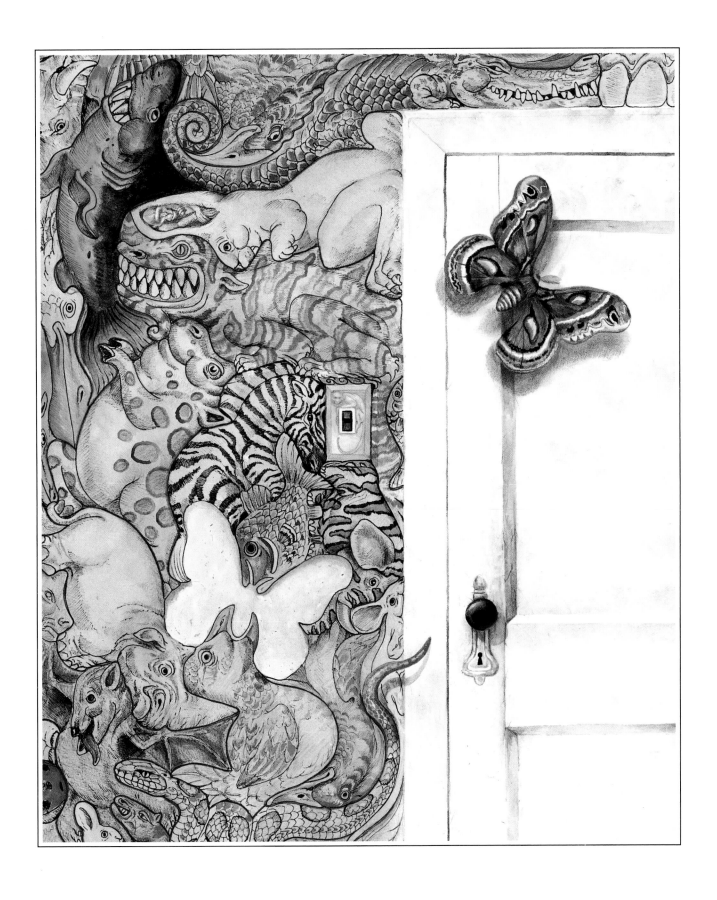

Having departed from her usual pattern,
Isadora seemed a little off-the-wall.

The MacRhino brothers, Angus and Skip,
would often lock horns over who got
to play the pipes.

As an artist, Nash was constantly looking for things to sink his teeth into.

While doing his famous wiggly dance,
the Amazing Schuman always tried to
put his best foot forward.

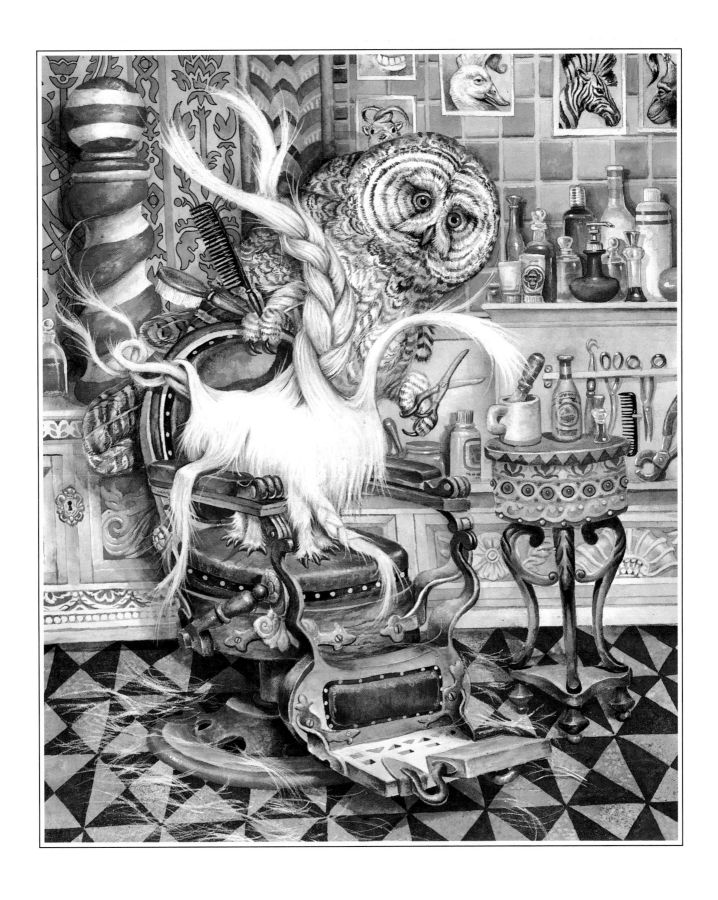

Despite his great skill as a barber, Hank couldn't make heads or tails out of some of his customers.

Snowflake had a strange feeling that someone was playing cat and mouse with her.

Willy seemed to attract misfortune,
but Bill was a lucky duck.

Byron had a lot on his mind, yet he couldn't think of a word to write.

Win or lose, when Bluebell raced Big
Daddy Jim she always had a whale
of a ride.

Although he blended in with the gang, Darnell was just a wolf in sheep's clothing.

When she realized she'd taken a wrong
turn, Gloria felt like a fish out of water.

After saying she wouldn't be hungry
if she missed lunch, Paige ended up
eating her words.

Every time the Bobzee twins bounced by, Old Zeke was reminded that he wasn't a spring chicken anymore.